Death of a Spaceman

Death of a Spaceman
Walter M. Miller, Jr.

ÆGYPAN PRESS

This novel first appeared in the March, 1954, issue of *Amazing Stories.*

Special thanks to Greg Weeks, Stephen Blundell, and the On-line Distributed Proofreading Team (which can be found at http://www.pgdp.net).

Death of a Spaceman
A publication of
ÆGYPAN PRESS

www.aegypan.com

The manner in which a man has lived is often the key to the way he will die. Take old man Donegal, for example. Most of his adult life was spent in digging a hole through space to learn what was on the other side. Would he go out the same way?

Old Donegal was dying. They had all known it was coming, and they watched it come — his haggard wife, his daughter, and now his grandson, home on emergency leave from the pre-astronautics academy. Old Donegal knew it too, and had known it from the beginning, when he had begun to lose control of his legs and was forced to walk with a cane. But most of the time, he pretended to let them keep the secret they shared with the doctors — that the operations had all been failures, and that the cancer that fed at his spine would gnaw its way brainward until the paralysis engulfed vital organs, and then Old Donegal would cease to be. It would be cruel to let them know that he knew. Once, weeks ago, he had joked about the approaching shadows.

"Buy the plot back where people won't walk over it, Martha," he said. "Get it way back under the cedars — next to the fence. There aren't many graves back there yet. I want to be alone."

"Don't *talk* that way, Donny!" his wife had choked. "You're not dying."

His eyes twinkled maliciously. "Listen, Martha, I want to be buried face-down. I want to be buried with my back to space, understand? Don't let them lay me out like a lily."

"Donny, *please!*"

"They oughta face a man the way he's headed," Donegal grunted. "I been up — *way* up. Now I'm going straight down."

Martha had fled from the room in tears. He had never done it again, except to the interns and nurses, who, while they insisted that he was going to get well, didn't mind joking with him about it.

Martha can bear my death, he thought, can bear pre-knowledge of it. But she couldn't bear thinking that he might take it calmly. If he accepted death gracefully, it would be like deliberately leaving her, and Old Donegal had decided to help her believe whatever would be comforting to her in such a troublesome moment.

"When'll they let me out of this bed again?" he complained.

"Be patient, Donny," she sighed. "It won't be long. You'll be up and around before you know it."

"Back on the moon-run, maybe?" he offered. "Listen, Martha, I been planet-bound too long. I'm not too old for the moon-run, am I? Sixty-three's not so old."

That had been carrying things too far. She knew he was hoaxing, and dabbed at her eyes again. The dead must humor the mourners, he thought, and the sick must comfort the visitors. It was always so.

But it was harder, now that the end was near. His eyes were hazy, and his thoughts unclear. He could move his arms a little, clumsily, but feeling was gone from them. The rest of his body was lost to him. Sometimes he seemed to feel his stomach and his hips, but the sensation was mostly an illusion offered by higher nervous centers, like the "ghost-arm" that an amputee continues to feel. The wires were down, and he was cut off from himself.

*H*e lay wheezing on the hospital bed, in his own room, in his own rented flat. Gaunt and unshaven, grey as winter twilight, he lay staring at the white net curtains that billowed gently in the breeze from the open window. There was no sound in the room but the sound of breathing and the loud ticking of an alarm clock. Occasionally he heard a chair scraping on the stone terrace next door, and the low mutter of voices, sometimes laughter, as the servants of the Keith mansion arranged the terrace for late afternoon guests.

With considerable effort, he rolled his head toward Martha who sat beside the bed, pinch-faced and weary.

"You ought to get some sleep," he said.

"I slept yesterday. Don't talk, Donny. It tires you."

"You ought to get more sleep. You never sleep enough. Are you afraid I'll get up and run away if you go to sleep for a while?"

She managed a brittle smile. "There'll be plenty of time for sleep when . . . when you're well again." The brittle smile fled and she swallowed hard, like swallowing a fish-bone. He glanced down, and noticed that she was squeezing his hand spasmodically.

There wasn't much left of the hand, he thought. Bones and ugly tight-stretched hide spotted with brown. Bulging knuckles with yellow cigaret stains. My hand. He tried to tighten it, tried to squeeze Martha's thin one in return. He watched it open and contract a little, but it was like operating a remote-control mechanism. Good-bye, hand, you're leaving me the way my legs did, he told it. I'll see you again in hell. How hammy can you get, Old Donegal? You maudlin ass.

"Requiescat," he muttered over the hand, and let it lie in peace.

Perhaps she heard him. "Donny," she whispered, leaning closer, "won't you let me call the priest now? Please."

He rattled a sigh and rolled his head toward the window again. "Are the Keiths having a party today?" he asked. "Sounds like they're moving chairs out on the terrace."

"Please, Donny, the priest?"

He let his head roll aside and closed his eyes, as if asleep. The bed shook slightly as she quickly caught at his wrist to feel for a pulse.

"If I'm not dying, I don't need a priest," he said sleepily.

"That's not right," she scolded softly. "You know that's not right, Donny. You know better."

Maybe I'm being too rough on her? he wondered. He hadn't minded getting baptized her way, and married her way, and occasionally priest-handled the way she wanted him to when he was home from a space-run, but when it came to dying, Old Donegal wanted to do it his own way.

*H*e opened his eyes at the sound of a bench being dragged across the stone terrace. "Martha, what kind of a party are the Keiths having today?"

"I wouldn't know," she said stiffly. "You'd think they'd have a little more respect. You'd think they'd put it off a few days."

"Until — ?"

"Until you feel better."

"I feel fine, Martha. I like parties. I'm glad they're having one. Pour me a drink, will you? I can't reach the bottle anymore."

"It's empty."

"No, it isn't, Martha, it's still a quarter full. I know. I've been watching it."

"You shouldn't have it, Donny. Please don't."

"But this is a party, Martha. Besides, the doctor says I can have whatever I want. Whatever I want, you hear? That means I'm getting well, doesn't it?"

"Sure, Donny, sure. Getting well."

"The whiskey, Martha. Just a finger in a tumbler, no more. I want to feel like it's a party."

Her throat was rigid as she poured it. She helped him get the tumbler to his mouth. The liquor seared his throat, and he gagged a little as the fumes clogged his nose. Good whiskey, the best — but he couldn't take it anymore. He eyed the green stamp on the neck of the bottle on the bed-table and grinned. He hadn't had whiskey like that since his space-days. Couldn't afford it now, not on a blastman's pension.

*H*e remembered how he and Caid used to smuggle a couple of fifths aboard for the moon-run. If they caught you, it meant suspension, but there was no harm in it, not for the blastroom men who had nothing much to do from the time the ship acquired enough velocity for the long, long coaster ride until they started the rockets again for Lunar landing. You could drink a fifth, jettison the bottle through the trash lock, and sober up before you were needed again. It was the only way to pass the time in the cramped cubicle, unless you ruined your eyes trying to read by the glow-lamps. Old Donegal chuckled. If he and Caid had stayed on the run, Earth would have a ring by now, like Saturn — a ring of Old Granddad bottles.

"You said it, Donny-boy," said the misty man by the billowing curtains. "Who else knows the gegenschein is broken glass?"

Donegal laughed. Then he wondered what the man was doing there. The man was lounging against the window, and his unzipped space rig draped about him in an old familiar way. Loose plug-in connections and hose-ends dangled about his lean body. He was freckled and grinning.

"Caid," Old Donegal breathed softly.

"What did you say, Donny?" Martha answered.

Old Donegal blinked hard and shook his head. Something let go with a soggy snap, and the misty man was gone. I'd better take it easy on the whiskey, he thought. You got to wait, Donegal, old lush, until Nora and Ken get here. You can't get drunk until they're gone, or you might get them mixed up with memories like Caid's.

Car doors slammed in the street below. Martha glanced toward the window.

"Think it's them? I wish they'd get here. I wish they'd hurry."

Martha arose and tiptoed to the window. She peered down toward the sidewalk, put on a sharp frown. He heard a distant mutter of voices and occasional laughter, with group-footsteps milling about on the sidewalk. Martha murmured her disapproval and closed the window.

"Leave it open," he said.

"But the Keiths' guests are starting to come. There'll be such a racket." She looked at him hopefully, the way she did when she prompted his manners before company came.

Maybe it wasn't decent to listen in on a party when you were dying, he thought. But that wasn't the reason. Donegal, your chamber-pressure's dropping off. Your brains are in your butt-end, where a spacer's brains belong, but your butt-end died last month. She wants the window closed for her own sake, not yours.

"Leave it closed," he grunted. "But open it again before the moon-run blasts off. I want to listen."

She smiled and nodded, glancing at the clock. "It'll be an hour and a half yet. I'll watch the time."

"I hate that clock. I wish you'd throw it out. It's loud."

"It's your medicine-clock, Donny." She came back to sit down at his bedside again. She sat in silence. The clock filled the room with its clicking pulse.

"What time are they coming?" he asked.

"Nora and Ken? They'll be here soon. Don't fret."

"Why should I fret?" He chuckled. "That boy — he'll be a good spacer, won't he, Martha?"

Martha said nothing, fanned at a fly that crawled across his pillow. The fly buzzed up in an angry spiral and alighted on the ceiling. Donegal watched it for a time. The fly had natural-born space-legs. I know your tricks, he told it with a smile, and I learned to walk on the bottomside of things before you were a maggot. You stand there with your magnasoles hanging to the hull, and the rest of you's in free fall. You jerk a sole loose, and your knee flies up to your belly, and reaction spins you half-around and near throws your other hip out of joint if you don't jam the foot down fast and jerk up the other. It's worse'n trying to run through knee-deep mud with snow-shoes, and a man'll go nuts trying to keep his arms and legs from taking off in odd directions. I know your tricks, fly. But the fly was born with his magnasoles, and he trotted across the ceiling like Donegal never could.

"That boy Ken — he ought to make a damn good space-engineer," wheezed the old man.

Her silence was long, and he rolled his head toward her again. Her lips tight, she stared down at the palm of his hand, unfolded his bony fingers, felt the cracked calluses that still welted the shrunken skin, calluses worn there by the linings of space gauntlets and the handles of fuel valves, and the rungs of get-about ladders during free fall.

"I don't know if I should tell you," she said.

"Tell me what, Martha?"

She looked up slowly, scrutinizing his face. "Ken's changed his mind, Nora says. Ken doesn't like the academy. She says he wants to go to medical school."

Old Donegal thought it over, nodded absently. "That's fine. Space-medics get good pay." He watched her carefully.

She lowered her eyes, rubbed at his calluses again. She shook her head slowly. "He doesn't want to go to space."

The clock clicked loudly in the closed room.

"I thought I ought to tell you, so you won't say anything to him about it," she added.

Old Donegal looked greyer than before. After a long silence, he rolled his head away and looked toward the limp curtains.

"Open the window, Martha," he said.

Her tongue clucked faintly as she started to protest, but she said nothing. After frozen seconds, she sighed and went to open it. The curtains billowed, and a babble of conversation blew in from the terrace of the Keith mansion. With the sound came the occasional brassy discord of a musician tuning his instrument. She clutched the window-sash as if she wished to slam it closed again.

"Well! Music!" grunted Old Donegal. "That's good. This is some shebang. Good whiskey and good music and you." He chuckled, but it choked off into a fit of coughing.

"Donny, about Ken —"

"No matter, Martha," he said hastily. "Space-medic's pay is good."

"But, Donny —" She turned from the window, stared at him briefly, then said, "Sure, Donny, sure," and came back to sit down by his bed.

He smiled at her affectionately. She was a man's woman, was Martha — always had been, still was. He had married her the year he had gone to space — a lissome, wistful, old-fashioned lass, with big violet eyes and gentle hands and gentle thoughts — and she had never complained about the long and lonely weeks between blast-off and glide-down, when most spacers' wives listened to the psychiatrists and soap-operas and soon developed the symptoms that were expected of them, either because the symptoms were *chic,* or because they felt they should do something to earn the pity that was extended to them. "It's not so bad," Martha had assured him. "The house keeps me busy till Nora's home from school, and then there's a flock of kids around till dinner. Nights are a little empty, but if there's a moon, I can always go out on the porch and look at it and know where you are. And Nora gets out the telescope you built her, and we make a game of it. 'Seeing if Daddy's still at the office,' she calls it."

"*T*hose were the days," he muttered.

"What, Donny?"

"Do you remember that Steve Farran song?"

She paused, frowning thoughtfully. There were a lot of Steve Farran songs, but after a moment she picked the right one, and sang it softly . . .

"O moon whereo'er the clouds fly,
  Beyond the willow tree,
  There is a ramblin' space guy
  I wish you'd save for me.

"Mare Tranquillitatis,
  O dark and tranquil sea,
  Until he drops from heaven,
  Rest him there with thee . . ."

Her voice cracked, and she laughed. Old Donegal chuckled weakly.

"Fried mush," he said. "That one made the cats wilt their ears and wail at the moon.

"I feel real crazy," he added. "Hand me the king kong, fluff-muff."

"Keep cool, Daddy-O, you've had enough." Martha reddened and patted his arm, looking pleased. Neither of them had talked that way, even in the old days, but the out-dated slang brought back memories — school parties, dances at the Rocketport Club, the early years of the war when Donegal had jockeyed an R-43 fighter in the close-space assaults against the Soviet satellite project. The memories were good.

A brassy blare of modern "slide" arose suddenly from the Keith terrace as the small orchestra launched into its first number. Martha caught an angry breath and started toward the window.

"Leave it," he said. "It's a party. Whiskey, Martha. Please — just a small one."

She gave him a hurtful glance.

"Whiskey. Then you can call the priest."

"Donny, it's not right. You know it's not right — to bargain for such as that."

"All right. Whiskey. Forget the priest."

She poured it for him, and helped him get it down, and then went out to make the phone-call. Old Donegal lay shuddering over the whiskey taste and savoring the burn in his throat. Jesus, but it was good.

You old bastard, he thought, you got no right to enjoy life when nine-tenths of you is dead already, and the rest is foggy as a thermal dust-rise on the lunar maria at hell-dawn. But it wasn't a bad way to die. It ate your consciousness away from the feet up; it gnawed away the Present, but it let you keep the Past, until everything faded and blended. Maybe that's what Eternity was, he thought — one man's subjective Past, all wrapped up and packaged for shipment, a single space-time entity, a one-man microcosm of memories, when nothing else remains.

"If I've got a soul, I made it myself," he told the grey nun at the foot of his bed.

The nun held out a pie pan, rattled a few coins in it. "Contribute to the Radiation Victims' Relief?" the nun purred softly.

"I know you," he said. "You're my conscience. You hang around the officers' mess, and when we get back from a sortie, you make us pay for the damage we did. But that was forty years ago."

The nun smiled, and her luminous eyes were on him softly. "Mother of God!" he breathed, and reached for the whiskey. His arm obeyed. The last drink had done him good. He had to watch his hand to see where it was going, and squeezed the neck until his fingers whitened so that he knew that he had it, but he got it off the table and onto his chest, and he got the cork out with his teeth. He had a long pull at the bottle, and it made his eyes water and his hands grow weak.

But he got it back to the table without spilling a bit, and he was proud of himself.

The room was spinning like the cabin of a gyro-grav-ved ship. By the time he wrestled it to a standstill, the nun was gone. The blare of music from the Keith terrace was louder, and laughing voices blended with it. Chairs scraping and glasses rattling. A fine party, Keith, I'm glad you picked today. This shebang would be the younger Keith's affair. Ronald Tonwyler Keith, III, scion of Orbital Engineering and Construction Company — builders of the moon-shuttle ships that made the run from the satellite station to Luna and back.

It's good to have such important neighbors, he thought. He wished he had been able to meet them while he was still up and about. But the Keiths' place was walled-in, and when a Keith came out, he charged out in a limousine with a chauffeur at the wheel, and the iron gate closed again. The Keiths built the wall when the surrounding neighborhood began to grow shabby with age. It had once been the best of neigh-borhoods, but that was before Old Donegal lived in it. Now it consisted of sooty old houses and rented flats, and the Keith place was really not a part of it anymore. Nevertheless, it was really something when a pensioned blastman could say, "I live out close to the Keiths — you know, the *Ronald* Keiths." At least, that's what Martha always told him.

The music was so loud that he never heard the doorbell ring, but when a lull came, he heard Nora's voice downstairs, and listened hopefully for Ken's. But when they came up, the boy was not with them.

"Hello, skinny-britches," he greeted his daughter.

Nora grinned and came over to kiss him. Her hair dangled about his face, and he noticed that it was blacker than usual, with the grey streaks gone from it again.

"You smell good," he said.

"You don't, Pops. You smell like a sot. Naughty!"

"Where's Ken?"

She moistened her lips nervously and looked away. "He couldn't come. He had to take a driver's lesson. He really couldn't help it. If he didn't go, he'd lose his turn, and then he wouldn't finish before he goes back to the academy." She looked at him apologetically.

"It's all right, Nora."

"If he missed it, he wouldn't get his copter license until summer."

"It's okay. Copters! Hell, the boy should be in jets by now!"

Several breaths passed in silence. She gazed absently toward the window and shook her head. "No jets, Pop. Not for Ken."

He glowered at her. "Listen! How'll he get into space? He's got to get his jet licenses first. Can't get in rockets without 'em."

Nora shot a quick glance at her mother. Martha rolled her eyes as if sighing patiently. Nora went to the window to stare down toward the Keith terrace. She tucked a cigaret between scarlet lips, lit it, blew nervous smoke against the pane.

"Mom, can't you call them and have that racket stopped?"

"Donny says he likes it."

Nora's eyes flitted over the scene below. "Female butterflies and puppy-dogs in sport jackets. And the cadets." She snorted. "Cadets! Imagine Ron Keith the Third ever going to space. The old man buys his way into the academy, and they throw a brawl as if Ronny passed the Compets."

"Maybe he did," growled Old Donegal.

"Hah!"

"They live in a different world, I guess," Martha sighed.

"If it weren't for men like Pops, they'd never've made their fortune."

"I like the music, I tell you," grumbled the old man.

"I'm half-a-mind to go over there and tell them off," Nora murmured.

"Let them alone. Just so they'll stop the racket for blast-away."

"Look at them! — polite little pattern-cuts, all alike. They take pre-space, because it's the thing to do. Then they quit before the pay-off comes."

"How do you know they'll quit?"

"That party — I bet it cost six months' pay, spacer's pay," she went on, ignoring him. "And what do real spacers get? Oley gets killed, and Pop's pension wouldn't feed the Keiths' cat."

"You don't understand, girl."

"I lost Oley. I understand enough."

*H*e watched her silently for a moment, then closed his eyes. It was no good trying to explain, no good trying to tell her the dough didn't mean a damn thing. She'd been a spacer's wife, and that was bad enough, but now she was a spacer's widow. And Oley? Oley's tomb revolved around the sun in an eccentric orbit that spun-in close to Mercury, then reached out into the asteroid belt, once every 725 days. When it came within rocket radius of Earth, it whizzed past at close to fifteen miles a second.

You don't rescue a ship like that, skinny-britches, my darling daughter. Nor do you salvage it after the crew stops screaming for help. If you use enough fuel to catch it, you won't get back. You just leave such a ship there forever, like an asteroid, and it's a damn shame about the men trapped aboard. Heroes all, no doubt — but the smallness of the widow's monthly check failed to confirm the heroism, and Nora was bitter about the price of Oley's memory, perhaps.

Ouch! Old Donegal, you know she's not like that. It's just that she can't understand about space. You ought to make her understand.

But did he really understand himself? You ride hot in a roaring blastroom, hands tense on the mixer controls and the pumps, eyes glued to instruments, body sucked down in a four-gravity thrust, and wait for the command to choke it off. Then you float free and weightless in a long nightmare as the beast coasts moonward, a flung javelin.

The "romance" of space — drivel written in the old days. When you're not blasting, you float in a cramped hotbox, crawl through dirty mazes of greasy pipe and cable to tighten a lug, scratch your arms and bark your shins, get sick and choked up because no gravity helps your gullet get the food down. Liquid is worse, but you gag your whiskey down because you have to.

Stars? — you see stars by squinting through a viewing lens, and it's like a photo-transparency, and if you aren't careful, you'll get an eyeful of Old Blinder and back off with a punch-drunk retina.

Adventure? — unless the skipper calls for course-correction, you float around in the blast-cubicle with damn little to do between blast-away and moon-down, except sweat out the omniscient accident statistics. If the beast blows up or gets gutted in space, a statistic had your name on it, that's all, and there's no fighting back. You stay outwardly sane because you're a hog for punishment; if you weren't, you'd never get past the psychologists.

"Did you like horror movies when you were a kid?" asked the psych. And you'd damn well better answer "yes," if you want to go to space.

*T*ell her, old man, you're her pop. Tell her why it's worth it, if you know. You jail yourself in a coffin-size cubicle, and a crazy beast thunders berserk for uncontrollable seconds, and then you soar in ominous silence for the long, long hours. Grow sweaty, filthy, sick, miserable, idle — somewhere out in Big Empty, where Man's got no business except the trouble he always makes for himself wherever he goes. Tell her why it's worth it, for pay less than a good bricklayer's. Tell her why Oley would do it again.

"It's a sucker's run, Nora," he said. "You go looking for kicks, but the only kicks you get to keep is what Oley got. God knows why — but it's worth it."

Nora said nothing. He opened his eyes slowly. Nora was gone. Had she been there at all?

He blinked around at the fuzzy room, and dissolved the shifting shadows that sometimes emerged as old friendly faces, grinning at him. He found Martha.

"You went to sleep," said Martha. "She had to go. Kennie called. He'll be over later, if you're not too tired."

"I'm not tired. I'm all head. There's nothing much to get tired."

"I love you, Old Donegal."

"Hold my hand again."

"I'm holding it, old man."

"Then hold me where I can feel it."

She slid a thin arm under his neck, and bent over his face to kiss him. She was crying a little, and he was glad she could do it now without fleeing the room.

"Can I talk about dying now?" he wondered aloud.

She pinched her lips together and shook her head.

"I lie to myself, Martha. You know how much I lie to myself?"

She nodded slowly and stroked his grey temples.

"I lie to myself about Ken, and about dying. If Ken turned spacer, I wouldn't die — that's what I told myself. You know?"

She shook her head. "Don't talk, Donny, please."

"A man makes his own soul, Martha."

"That's not true. You shouldn't say things like that."

"A man makes his own soul, but it dies with him, unless he can pour it into his kids and his grandchildren before he goes. I lied to myself. Ken's a yellow-belly. Nora made him one, and the boots won't fit."

"Don't, Donny. You'll excite yourself again."

"I was going to give him the boots — the overboots with magnasoles. But they won't fit him. They won't ever fit him. He's a lily-livered lap dog, and he whines. Bring me my boots, woman."

"Donny!"

"The boots, they're in my locker in the attic. I want them."

"What on earth!"

"Bring me my goddam space boots and put them on my feet. I'm going to wear them."

"You can't; the priest's coming."

"Well, get them anyway. What time is it? You didn't let me sleep through the moon-run blast, did you?"

She shook her head. "It's half an hour yet . . . I'll get the boots if you promise not to make me put them on you."

"I want them on."

"You can't, until Father Paul's finished."

"Do I have to get my feet buttered?"

She sighed. "I wish you wouldn't say things like that. I wish you wouldn't, Donny. It's sacrilege, you know it is."

"All right — 'anointed'," he corrected wearily.

"Yes, you do."

"The boots, woman, the boots."

She went to get them. While she was gone, the doorbell rang, and he heard her quick footsteps on the stairs, and then Father Paul's voice asking about the patient. Old Donegal groaned inwardly. After the priest, the doctor would come, at the usual time, to see if he were dead yet. The doctor had let him come home from the hospital to die, and the doctor was getting impatient. Why don't they let me alone? he growled. Why don't they let me handle it in my own way, and stop making a fuss over it? I can die and do a good job of it without a lot of outside interference, and I wish they'd quit picking at me with syringes and sacraments and enemas. All he wanted was a chance to listen to the orchestra on the Keith terrace, to drink the rest of his whiskey, and to hear the beast blast-away for the satellite on the first lap of the run to Luna.

*I*t's going to be my last day, he thought. My eyes are going fuzzy, and I can't breathe right, and the throbbing's hurting my head. Whether he lived through the night wouldn't matter, because delirium was coming over him, and then there would be the coma, and the symbolic fight to keep him pumping and panting. I'd rather die tonight and get it over with, he thought, but they probably won't let me go.

He heard their voices coming up the stairs . . .

"Nora tried to get them to stop it, Father, but she couldn't get in to see anybody but the butler. He told her he'd tell Mrs. Keith, but nothing happened. It's just as loud as before."

"Well, as long as Donny doesn't mind —"

"He just says that. You know how he is."

"What're they celebrating, Martha?"

"Young Ronald's leaving — for pre-space training. It's a going-away affair." They paused in the doorway. The small priest smiled in at Donegal and nodded. He set his black bag on the floor inside, winked solemnly at the patient.

"I'll leave you two alone," said Martha. She closed the door and her footsteps wandered off down the hall.

Donegal and the young priest eyed each other warily.

"You look like hell, Donegal," the padre offered jovially. "Feeling nasty?"

"Skip the small talk. Let's get this routine over with."

The priest humphed thoughtfully, sauntered across to the bed, gazed down at the old man disinterestedly. "What's the matter? Don't want the 'routine'? Rather play it tough?"

"What's the difference?" he growled. "Hurry up and get out. I want to hear the beast blast off."

"You won't be able to," said the priest, glancing at the window, now closed again. "That's quite a racket next door."

"They'd better stop for it. They'd better quiet down for it. They'll have to turn it off for five minutes or so."

"Maybe they won't."

It was a new idea, and it frightened him. He liked the music, and the party's gaiety, the nearness of youth and good times — but it hadn't occurred to him that it wouldn't stop so he could hear the beast.

"Don't get upset, Donegal. You know what a blast-off sounds like."

"But it's the last one. The last time. I want to hear."

"How do you know it's the last time?"

"Hell, don't I know when I'm kicking off?"

"Maybe, maybe not. It's hardly your decision."

"It's not, eh?" Old Donegal fumed. "Well, bigawd you'd think it wasn't. You'd think it was Martha's and yours and that damfool medic's. You'd think I got no say-so. Who's doing it anyway?"

"I would guess," Father Paul grunted sourly, "that Providence might appreciate His fair share of the credit."

Old Donegal made a surly noise and hunched his head back into the pillow to glower.

"You want me?" the priest asked. "Or is this just a case of wifely conscience?"

"What's the difference? Give me the business and scram."

"No soap. Do you want the sacrament, or are you just being kind to your wife? If it's for Martha, I'll go *now.*"

Old Donegal glared at him for a time, then wilted. The priest brought his bag to the bedside.

"Bless me, father, for I have sinned."

"Bless you, son."

"I accuse myself . . ."

*T*ension, anger, helplessness — they had piled up on him, and now he was feeling the after-effects. Vertigo, nausea, and the black confetti — a bad spell. The whiskey — if he could only reach the whiskey. Then he remembered he was receiving a Sacrament, and struggled to get on with it. Tell him, old man, tell him of your various rottennesses and vile transgressions, if you can remember some. A sin is whatever you're sorry for, maybe. But Old Donegal, you're sorry for the wrong things, and this young jesuitical gadget wouldn't like listening to it. I'm sorry I didn't get it instead of Oley, and I'm sorry I fought in the war, and I'm sorry I can't get out of this bed and take a belt to my daughter's backside for making a puny whelp out of Ken, and I'm sorry I gave Martha such a rough time all these years — and wound up dying in a cheap flat, instead of giving her things like the Keiths had. I wish I had been a sharpster, contractor, or thief ... instead of a common laboring spacer, whose species lost its glamour after the war.

Listen, old man, you made your soul yourself, and it's yours. This young dispenser of oils, substances, and mysteries wishes only to help you scrape off the rough edges and gouge out the bad spots. He will not steal it, nor distort it with his supernatural chisels, nor make fun of it. He can take nothing away, but only cauterize and neutralize, he says, so why not let him try? Tell him the rotten messes.

"Are you finished, my son?"

Old Donegal nodded wearily, and said what he was asked to say, and heard the soft mutter of Latin that washed him inside and behind his ghostly ears ... *ego te absolvo in Nomine Patris* ... and he accepted the rest of it lying quietly in the candlelight and the red glow of the sunset through the window, while the priest anointed him and gave him bread, and read the words of the soul in greeting its spouse: "I was asleep, but my heart waked; it is the voice of my beloved calling: come to me my love, my dove, my undefiled ..." and from beyond the closed window came the sarcastic wail of a clarinet painting hot slides against a rhythmic background.

It wasn't so bad, Old Donegal thought when the priest was done. He felt like a schoolboy in a starched shirt on Sunday morning, and it wasn't a bad feeling, though it left him weak.

The priest opened the window for him again, and repacked his bag. "Ten minutes till blast-off," he said. "I'll see what I can do about the racket next door."

When he was gone, Martha came back in, and he looked at her face and was glad. She was smiling when she kissed him, and she looked less tired.

"Is it all right for me to die now?" he grunted.

"Donny, don't start that again."

"Where's the boots? You promised to bring them?"

"They're in the hall. Donny, you don't want them."

"I want them, and I want a drink of whiskey, and I want to hear them fire the beast." He said it slow and hard, and he left no room for argument.

When she had got the huge boots over his shrunken feet, the magnasoles clanged against the iron bedframe and clung there, and she rolled him up so that he could look at them, and Old Donegal chuckled inside. He felt warm and clean and pleasantly dizzy.

"The whiskey, Martha, and for God's sake, make them stop the noise till after the firing. Please!"

She went to the window and looked out for a long time. Then she came back and poured him an insignificant drink.

"Well?"

"I don't know," she said. "I saw Father Paul on the terrace, talking to somebody."

"Is it time?"

She glanced at the clock, looked at him doubtfully, and nodded. "Nearly time."

The orchestra finished a number, but the babble of laughing voices continued. Old Donegal sagged. "They won't do it. They're the Keiths, Martha. Why should I ruin their party?"

She turned to stare at him, slowly shook her head. He heard someone shouting, but then a trumpet started softly, introducing a new number. Martha sucked in a hurt breath, pressed her hands together, and hurried from the room.

"It's too late," he said after her.

Her footsteps stopped on the stairs. The trumpet was alone. Donegal listened; and there was no babble of voices, and the rest of the orchestra was silent. Only the trumpet sang — and it puzzled him, hearing the same slow bugle-notes of the call played at the lowering of the colors.

The trumpet stopped suddenly. Then he knew it had been for him.

A brief hush — then thunder came from the blast-station two miles to the west. First the low reverberation, rattling the windows, then the rising growl as the sleek beast knifed skyward on a column of blue-white hell. It grew and grew until it drowned the distant traffic sounds and dominated the silence outside.

Quit crying, you old fool, you maudlin ass . . .

"My boots," he whispered, "my boots . . . please . . ."

"You've got them on, Donny."

He sank quietly then. He closed his eyes and let his heart go up with the beast, and he sank into the gravity padding of the blastroom, and Caid was with him, and Oley. And when Ronald Keith, III, instructed the orchestra to play Blastroom Man, after the beast's rumble had waned, Old Donegal was on his last moon-run, and he was grinning. He'd had a good day.

Martha went to the window to stare out at the thin black trail that curled starward above the blast-station through the twilight sky. Guests on the terrace were watching it too.

The doorbell rang. That would be Ken, too late. She closed the window against the chill breeze, and went

back to the bed. The boots, the heavy, clumsy boots —
they clung to the bedframe, with his feet half out of
them. She took them off gently and set them out of
company's sight. Then she went to answer the door.

www.ingramcontent.com/pod-product-compliance
Lightning Source LLC
Chambersburg PA
CBHW031905170626
46807CB00004B/1912